Delicious!

For Pandora and Laura and Greg, who have shared many meals.

DEDICATION

Annie Eaton

Ian Butterworth

SECRET INGREDIENTS

Delicious!

Helen Cooper

Farrar Straus Giroux / New York

Deep in the woods it was lunchtime,
munchtime,
should have been cooking time,
down at the old white cabin.

But out in the garden there was rustling,
and scuffling,
a bit of a kerfuffling.
The sound of a Duck
and a Squirrel
and a Cat,
looking for a pumpkin in the pumpkin patch.

They couldn't find a single ripe one.

Pumpkin Soup,
all they ever wanted,
all they ever cooked in the old white cabin.
"We might have to make something different today,"
they agreed.

Back at the cabin, the Cat pulled down
a faded old recipe book.
They blew off the cobwebs
and, turning the pages,
they wondered what else they could cook.

"Fish Soup!" said the Cat. "That sounds **scrumptious!**"
"Nutritious!" said the Squirrel.
"Delicious?" said the Duck.

So they all went fishing,
and that afternoon
the Duck caught four little minnows.

The Squirrel caught only a cold.

But the Cat caught twenty-two
beautiful trout, and they
brought them back to
the old white cabin.

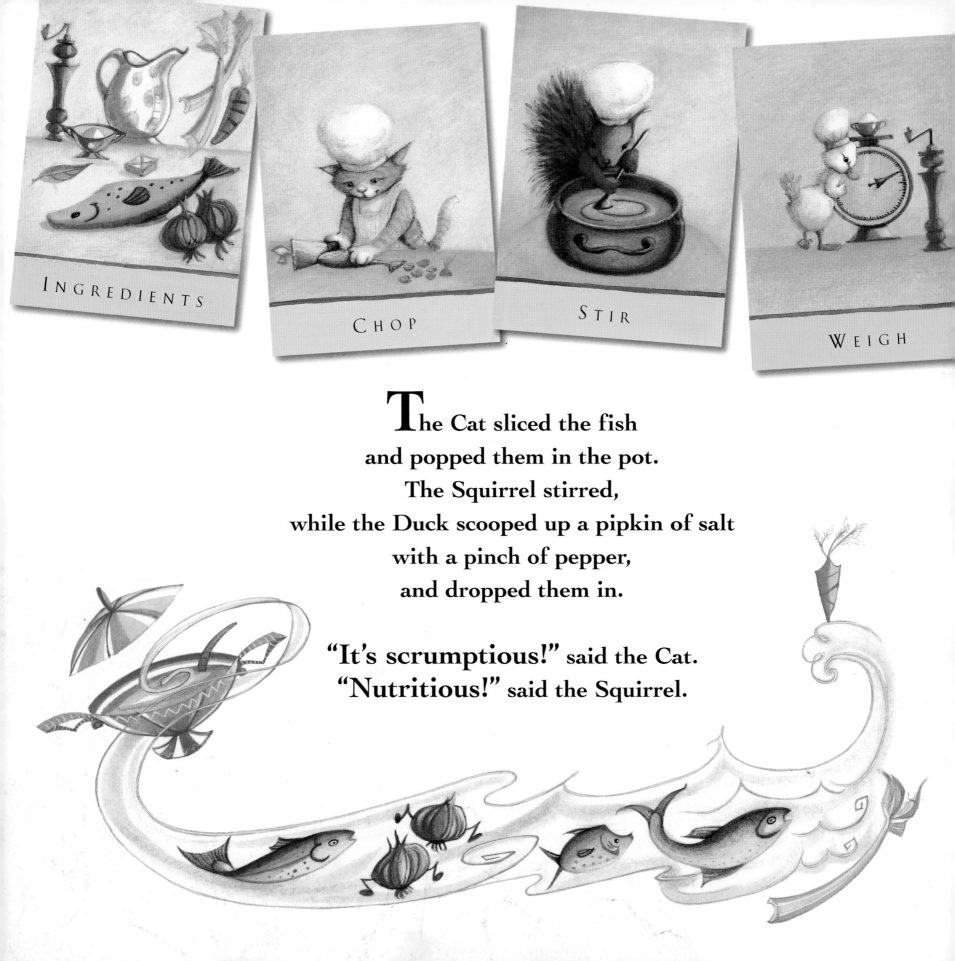

INGREDIENTS

CHOP

STIR

WEIGH

The Cat sliced the fish
and popped them in the pot.
The Squirrel stirred,
while the Duck scooped up a pipkin of salt
with a pinch of pepper,
and dropped them in.

"It's scrumptious!" said the Cat.
"Nutritious!" said the Squirrel.

But the Duck sniffed the soup and said,

"YUCK!"

He wouldn't even try it.

Fish Soup.

The best you ever tasted?

Most of the soup was going to be wasted.

They turned the pages of their recipe book

and wondered what else they could cook.

"**Mushroom Soup,**" said the Squirrel.

"That sounds **scrumptious!**"

Fig II

Agaricus campestris

Fig III

Fig IV

So they all went mushrooming.

Soon the Duck found a toadstool.

The Cat found something worse.

But the Squirrel found a mound of mushrooms.
And they carried them back to the old white cabin.

M ushroom Soup.
Would it be wasted?
Time for the Mushroom Soup to be tasted.

"Scrumptious!" squeaked the Squirrel.
"Nutritious?" said the Cat.
But the Duck sniffed the soup and said,

"YUCK!"

He wouldn't even try it.

He went to bed feeling hungry,
with horrible pains in his tummy,
and dreamed of Spider Soup.

WOODWORM
BUILDING
Co-op

At peep of dawn, there was no peace
for the Cat and Squirrel,
trying to sleep in the old white cabin.
The Duck was hunting for a pumpkin,
hoping one had ripened.
"All I want is Pumpkin Soup," he mumbled,
and his hungry tummy rumbled,
and he began to cry.

The Cat remembered it was market day.
"Perhaps we could buy a pumpkin," he said.

"Let's go!" quacked the Duck, and he ran off ahead with the basket.

At the woodland market there were vegetable stalls,
heaped tall
with peas
and beans
and eggplants
and onions
and parsnips.
Sadly, not a pumpkin to be seen.

And soon the Duck grumbled that his feet were sore,
and he cried, and he fussed, and he whined to go home.

"Buy something, quick!" said the Cat.
So the Squirrel bought some beets.

"They're brown and ugly!"
bawled the Duck.
But the Cat and the Squirrel were ready to leave.

WOODWORM
BUILDING
Co-op

Home in the cabin,
the Cat peeled the beets
and sliced them
and popped them in the pot,
while the Squirrel stirred.
And it looked pretty good!
The Duck didn't help.
He lay in bed with a headache.

That's what happens when you don't eat.

Beet Soup.
The best you ever tasted.
Made by the Cat and the Squirrel
for the Duck,
who took one look and said . . .

Stand by for soup!

okey dokey

"I'm not eating that. It's pink!"

"You deserve to starve!"
growled the Squirrel.
"But all I want is Pumpkin Soup,"
howled the Duck.
"And that's orange!"

Then there was trouble.
A horrible squabble,
a hullabaloo in the old white cabin.

"**I**'ll trick him," whispered the Cat.

While the others ran a bath,
he slipped away with the basket again.
This time he bought some yellow zucchini,
the ripest tomatoes,
carrots,
and corn.

When no one was watching, he peeled them

and sliced them

and chopped them

and diced them

and squished them

and plopped them

into the cooking pot.

"That ought to do," he said to himself.
"Exactly the color of Pumpkin Soup."

The Duck peered into the cooking pot.
"That looks like Pumpkin Soup!" he said.
He rushed to scoop up a pipkin of salt with a pinch of pepper
and dropped them in, while the Squirrel stirred.

They all stirred,

and soon it was soup-slurping time.

"Scrumptious?" said the Cat.

"Nutritious?" said the Squirrel.

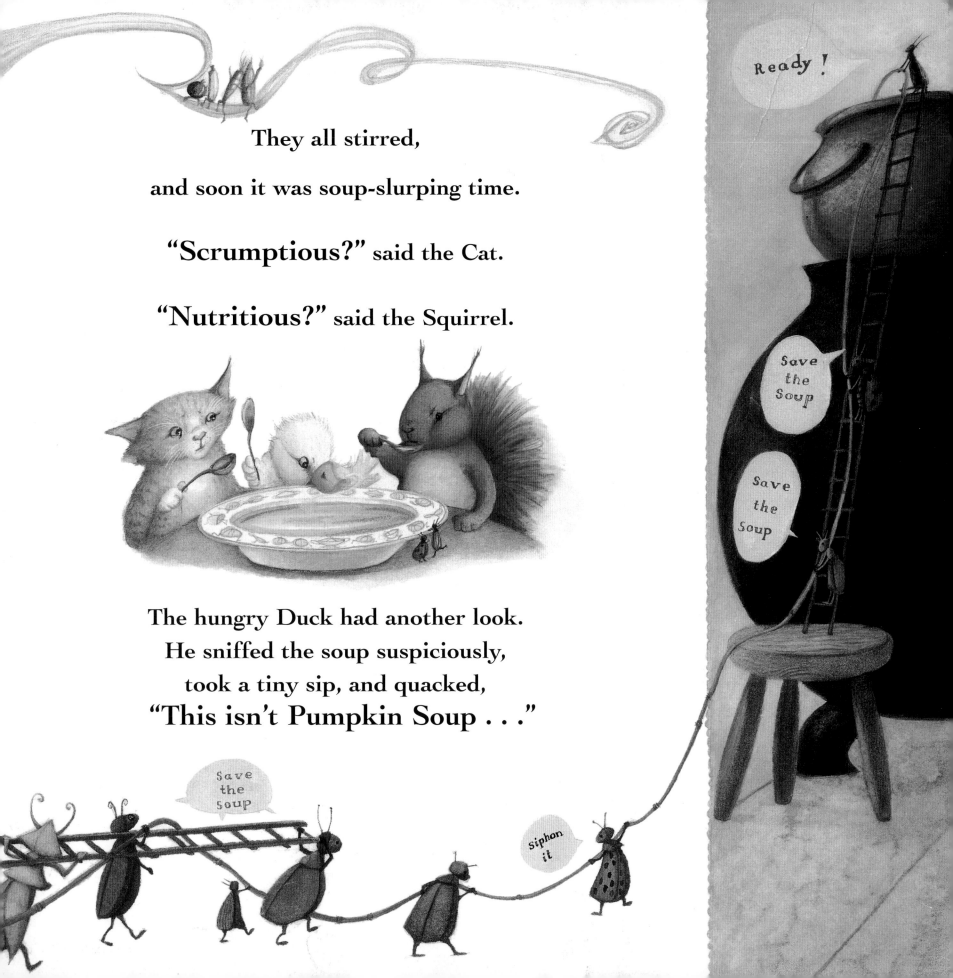

The hungry Duck had another look.
He sniffed the soup suspiciously,
took a tiny sip, and quacked,
"This isn't Pumpkin Soup . . ."